A NOTE TO PARENTS

Reading is one of the most important gifts we can give our children. How can you help your child to become interested in reading? By reading aloud!

My First Games Readers make excellent read-alouds and are the very first books your child will be able to read by him/herself. Based on the games children know and love, the goals of these books include helping your child:

- **learn sight words**
- **understand that print corresponds to speech**
- **understand that words are read from left to right and top to bottom**

Here are some tips on how to read together and how to enjoy the fun activities in the back of these books:

Reading Together

- Set aside a special time each day to read to your child. Encourage your child to comment on the story or pictures or predict what might happen next.
- After reading the book, you might wish to start lists of words that begin with a specific letter (such as the first letter of your child's name) or words your child would like to learn.
- Ask your child to read these books on his/her own. Have your child read to you while you are preparing dinner or driving to the grocery store.

Reading Activities

- The activities listed in the back of this book are designed to use and expand what children know through reading and writing. You may choose to do one activity a night, following each reading of the book.
- Keep the activities gamelike and don't forget to praise your child's efforts!

Whatever you do, have fun with this book as you pass along the joy of reading to your child. It's a gift that will last a lifetime!

Wiley Blevins, Reading Specialist
Ed.M. Harvard University

ISBN 0-439-23564-2

Copyright © 2000 by Hasbro Inc.

CHUTES AND LADDERS® is a registered trademark of Hasbro Inc.
All rights reserved. Published by Scholastic Inc.

SCHOLASTIC and associated logos are trademarks and/or registered trademarks of Scholastic Inc.

12 11 10 9 8 7 6 5 4 3 2 1   0 1 2 3 4 5 6/0

Illustrated by Suwin Chan
Designed by Peter Koblish

Printed in the U.S.A.
First Scholastic printing, December 2000

my first
games
readers

Chutes and Ladders®
Play Day

by Jackie Glassman
Illustrated by Suwin Chan

SCHOLASTIC INC.

New York   Toronto   London   Auckland   Sydney   Mexico City   New Delhi   Hong Kong

Today is play day!

Hold on!

It is fun to go up and down.

Here I go.

That hurts!

Come play with us!

Thank you for playing with me.

I am getting off.

Ouch!

Come here, kitty.

Thank you!

All done!

Oh, no!

Share my cookie.

This is good!

What pretty flowers!

Where are the flowers?

My kite is stuck!

Look at the kite fly!

What Happened?

On a separate piece of paper, match each picture in column A to a picture in column B to show what happened in the story.

A	**B**

Fix It!

On a separate piece of paper, draw and tell how you would fix each of these problems.

Rhyme Lines

In each line, name the pictures
to make a rhyme.

Here are pictures of kids from the story.
Each one is doing something nice.
On a piece of paper, draw a picture
of another kid doing something nice.

S Is For . . .

Which of these begins with the letter *S*?

Double Trouble

Can you find the twins in this playground?

About Face!

Here are some pictures of the kids from the story. Look at their faces and tell what you think they are feeling.

Silly, Mixed-Up Playground

Look at this picture of a silly, mixed-up playground. Find everything that is wrong.

Answers

What Happened?

S Is For . . .

These begin with *S*:

Silly, Mixed-Up Playground

Double Trouble

Here are the twin girls.

Rhyme Lines

I see a **FLY** in the **SKY**.

I see a **HAND** in the **SAND**

I see a **BEE** near the **TREE**